MW01115577

WOULD RATHER ?

9 YEAR OLD
VERSION

FOLLOW US AT:

f **WWW.FACEBOOK.COM/
WOULDYOURATHERBOOK** **f**

 **@WOULDYOURATHERBOOK**

WWW.WOULDYOURATHERBOOK.COM

COME
JOIN OUR GROUP

GET A BONUS PDF PACKED WITH HILARIOUS JOKES, AND THINGS TO MAKE YOU SMILE!

GO TO:

https://bit.ly/3n9Nj5u

■ **Get a Bonus fun PDF** (filled with jokes, and fun would you rather questions)

■ *Get entered into our monthly competition to win a $100 Amazon gift card*

■ *Hear about our up and coming new books*

HOW TO PLAY?

You can play to win or play for fun, the choice is yours!

1. Player 1 asks player 2 to either choose questions **A** or **B**.

2. Then player 1 reads out the chosen questions.

3. Player 2 decides on an answer to their dilemma, and either memorize their answer or notes it down.

4. Player 1 has to guess player 2's answer. If they guess correctly they win a point, if not player 2 wins a point.

5. Take turns asking the questions, **the first to 7 points wins.**

(Note: It can be fun to do funny voices or make silly faces)

REMEMBER
Do **NOT** ATTEMPT TO DO ANY OF THE SCENARIOS IN THIS BOOK, THEY ARE ONLY MEANT FOR FUN!

WOULD YOU RATHER?
9 YEAR OLD
VERSION

PLAYER 1

(ASK THE OTHER PLAYER(S) TO
CHOOSE QUESTION 1 OR QUESTION 2)

A — WOULD YOU RATHER

HAVE A WART ON YOUR FACE

OR

FIVE WARTS ON YOUR HANDS?

B — WOULD YOU RATHER

BE A PILOT

OR

A PIRATE?

WOULD YOU RATHER ?

9 YEAR OLD
VERSION

PLAYER 2

(ASK THE OTHER PLAYER(S) TO
CHOOSE QUESTION 1 OR QUESTION 2)

A WOULD YOU RATHER

HAVE YOUR MOM COME TO SCHOOL FOR THE DAY

 OR

GO TO WORK WITH HER FOR THE DAY?

B WOULD YOU RATHER

HAVE ONE HUNDRED BIRDS SINGING IN YOUR GARDEN EARLY IN THE MORNING

 OR

ONE HUNDRED CATS MIAOWING?

WOULD YOU RATHER?
9 YEAR OLD
VERSION

PLAYER 1

(ASK THE OTHER PLAYER(S) TO
CHOOSE QUESTION 1 OR QUESTION 2)

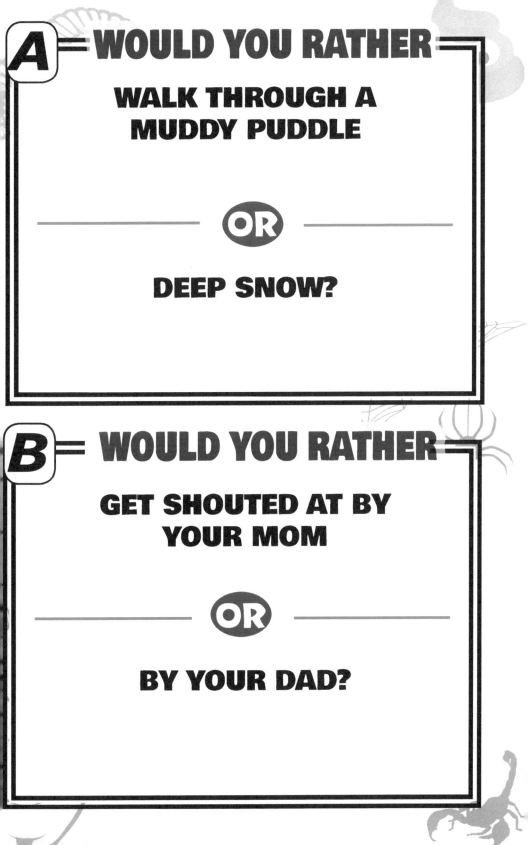

A WOULD YOU RATHER

WALK THROUGH A MUDDY PUDDLE

OR

DEEP SNOW?

B WOULD YOU RATHER

GET SHOUTED AT BY YOUR MOM

OR

BY YOUR DAD?

WOULD YOU RATHER?

9 YEAR OLD
VERSION

PLAYER 2

(ASK THE OTHER PLAYER(S) TO
CHOOSE QUESTION 1 OR QUESTION 2)

A WOULD YOU RATHER

LIVE IN A TENT

 OR

LIVE IN A TREE?

B WOULD YOU RATHER

POOP IN A BUCKET

 OR

POOP IN A HOLE IN THE GROUND?

WOULD YOU RATHER?
9 YEAR OLD
VERSION

PLAYER 1

(ASK THE OTHER PLAYER(S) TO
CHOOSE QUESTION 1 OR QUESTION 2)

WOULD YOU RATHER

LISTEN TO MUSIC YOU DON'T LIKE

 OR

LISTEN TO NO MUSIC?

WOULD YOU RATHER

PLAY FOOTBALL

 OR

PLAY BASKETBALL?

WOULD YOU RATHER ?

9 YEAR OLD
VERSION

PLAYER 2

(ASK THE OTHER PLAYER(S) TO
CHOOSE QUESTION 1 OR QUESTION 2)

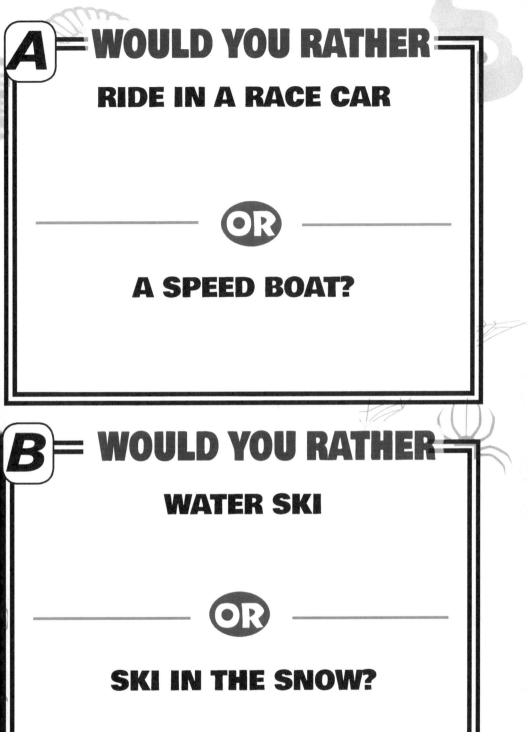

A WOULD YOU RATHER

RIDE IN A RACE CAR

OR

A SPEED BOAT?

B WOULD YOU RATHER

WATER SKI

OR

SKI IN THE SNOW?

WOULD YOU RATHER?
9 YEAR OLD
VERSION

PLAYER 1

(ASK THE OTHER PLAYER(S) TO
CHOOSE QUESTION 1 OR QUESTION 2)

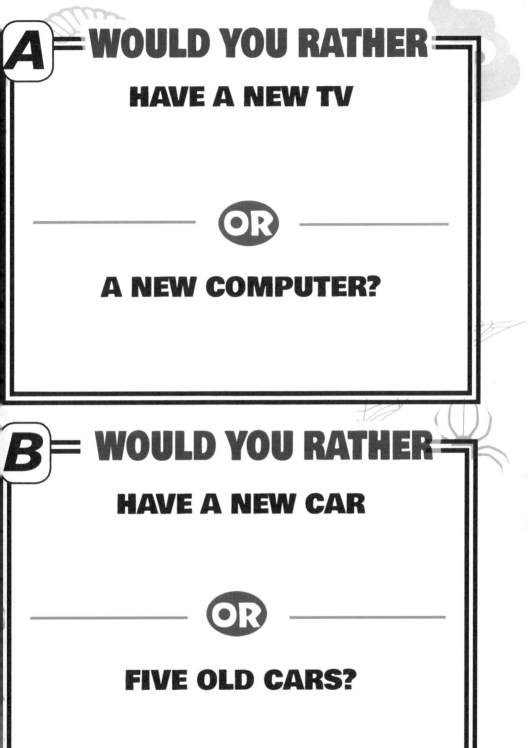

WOULD YOU RATHER?

9 YEAR OLD
VERSION

PLAYER 2

(ASK THE OTHER PLAYER(S) TO
CHOOSE QUESTION 1 OR QUESTION 2)

A WOULD YOU RATHER

READ COMICS

 OR

A BABY FILM?

B WOULD YOU RATHER

BE ABLE TO GO ON A ROLLERCOASTER

 OR

A FERRIS WHEEL?

WOULD YOU RATHER ?
9 YEAR OLD
VERSION

PLAYER 1

(ASK THE OTHER PLAYER(S) TO
CHOOSE QUESTION 1 OR QUESTION 2)

A WOULD YOU RATHER

SMELL ROTTEN EGGS

OR

YOUR DAD'S FARTS?

B WOULD YOU RATHER

EAT A HOTDOG

OR

EAT A HAMBURGER?

WOULD YOU RATHER?
9 YEAR OLD
VERSION

PLAYER 2

(ASK THE OTHER PLAYER(S) TO
CHOOSE QUESTION 1 OR QUESTION 2)

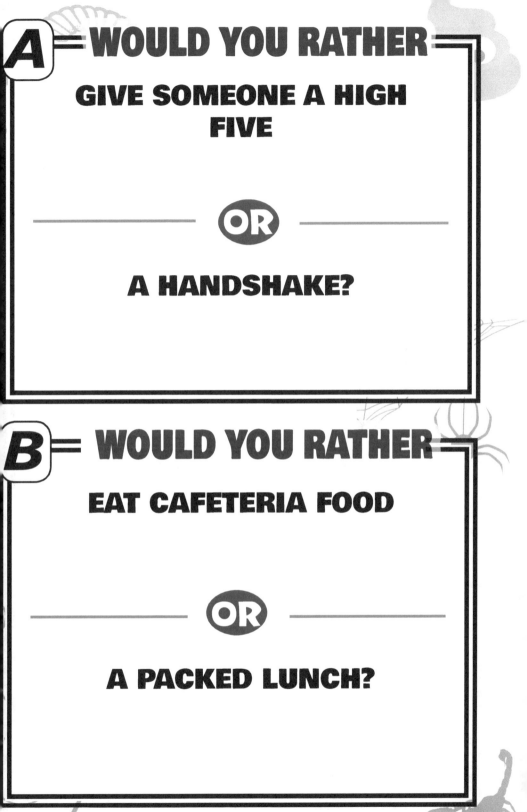

A — WOULD YOU RATHER

GIVE SOMEONE A HIGH FIVE

OR

A HANDSHAKE?

B — WOULD YOU RATHER

EAT CAFETERIA FOOD

OR

A PACKED LUNCH?

WOULD YOU RATHER?

9 YEAR OLD
VERSION

PLAYER 1

(ASK THE OTHER PLAYER(S) TO
CHOOSE QUESTION 1 OR QUESTION 2)

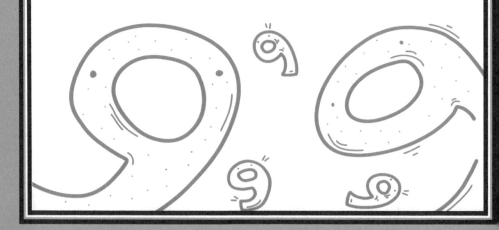

A — WOULD YOU RATHER

GO HOME FOR LUNCH EVERY DAY

 OR

STAY AT SCHOOL WITH YOUR FRIENDS?

B — WOULD YOU RATHER

FIND YOURSELF STUCK IN A TINY ROOM WITH NO FURNITURE BUT WITH YOUR BEST FRIEND

 OR

IN A BIG ROOM WITH COMFORTABLE FURNITURE BUT ON YOUR OWN?

WOULD YOU RATHER ?
9 YEAR OLD
VERSION

PLAYER 2

(ASK THE OTHER PLAYER(S) TO
CHOOSE QUESTION 1 OR QUESTION 2)

A WOULD YOU RATHER

EAT FISH

 OR

EAT CHICKEN?

B WOULD YOU RATHER

BE STUCK WITH A RUNNY NOSE

 OR

A COUGH?

WOULD YOU RATHER?

9 YEAR OLD
VERSION

PLAYER 1

(ASK THE OTHER PLAYER(S) TO
CHOOSE QUESTION 1 OR QUESTION 2)

WOULD YOU RATHER

A

HAVE A BOUNCY CASTLE

 OR

A BALL PIT IN YOUR GARDEN?

WOULD YOU RATHER

B

GO ON A ZIP LINE

 OR

GO ON A WATER SLIDE?

WOULD YOU RATHER ?

9 YEAR OLD
VERSION

PLAYER 2

(ASK THE OTHER PLAYER(S) TO
CHOOSE QUESTION 1 OR QUESTION 2)

A | WOULD YOU RATHER

HAVE ABSOLUTELY NO HAIR AT ALL

 OR

BE COMPLETELY COVERED IN HAIR?

B | WOULD YOU RATHER

WEAR A DIAPER

 OR

DRINK FROM A BABY BOTTLE?

WOULD YOU RATHER?

9 YEAR OLD
VERSION

PLAYER 1

(ASK THE OTHER PLAYER(S) TO
CHOOSE QUESTION 1 OR QUESTION 2)

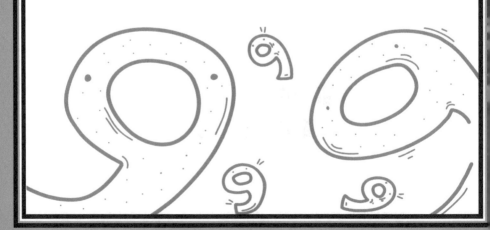

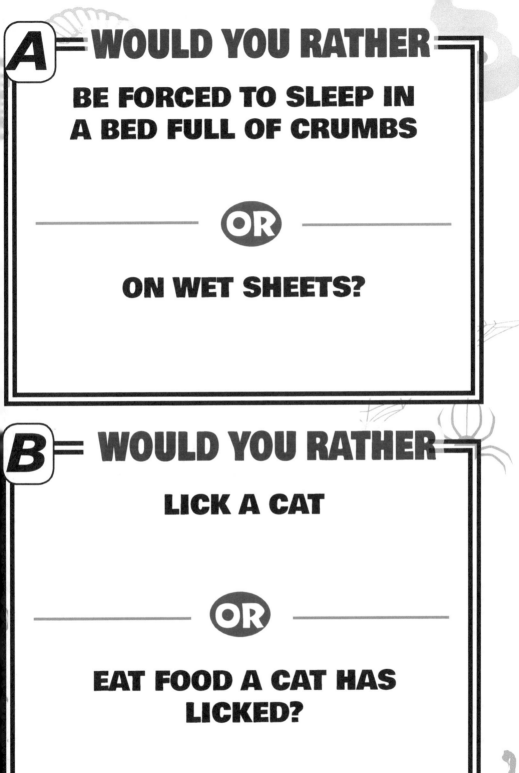

A | WOULD YOU RATHER

BE FORCED TO SLEEP IN A BED FULL OF CRUMBS

OR

ON WET SHEETS?

B | WOULD YOU RATHER

LICK A CAT

OR

EAT FOOD A CAT HAS LICKED?

WOULD YOU RATHER?
9 YEAR OLD
VERSION

PLAYER 2

(ASK THE OTHER PLAYER(S) TO
CHOOSE QUESTION 1 OR QUESTION 2)

A — WOULD YOU RATHER

HOLD AN OCTOPUS?

 OR

WEAR SHOES THAT ARE TOO SMALL

B — WOULD YOU RATHER

UNDERWEAR THAT IS TOO SMALL?

 OR

HAVE HAIR LIKE YOUR GRANDMOTHER

WOULD YOU RATHER?
9 YEAR OLD
VERSION

PLAYER 1

(ASK THE OTHER PLAYER(S) TO
CHOOSE QUESTION 1 OR QUESTION 2)

WOULD YOU RATHER

A HORSE'S TAIL

OR

HAVE A HORSE'S HOOVES?

WOULD YOU RATHER

HAVE A COLD SHOWER

OR

HAVE AN HOUR LESS IN BED EVERY MORNING?

WOULD YOU RATHER ?

9 YEAR OLD
VERSION

PLAYER 2

(ASK THE OTHER PLAYER(S) TO
CHOOSE QUESTION 1 OR QUESTION 2)

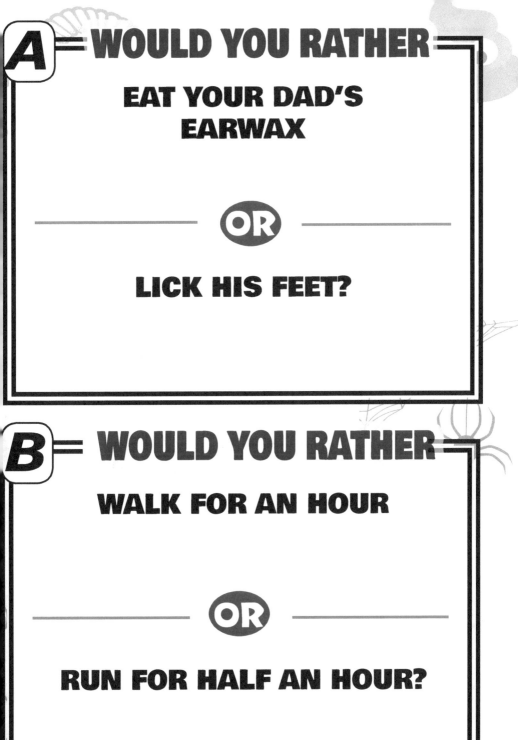

A WOULD YOU RATHER

EAT YOUR DAD'S EARWAX

OR

LICK HIS FEET?

B WOULD YOU RATHER

WALK FOR AN HOUR

OR

RUN FOR HALF AN HOUR?

WOULD YOU RATHER?

9 YEAR OLD
VERSION

PLAYER 1

(ASK THE OTHER PLAYER(S) TO
CHOOSE QUESTION 1 OR QUESTION 2)

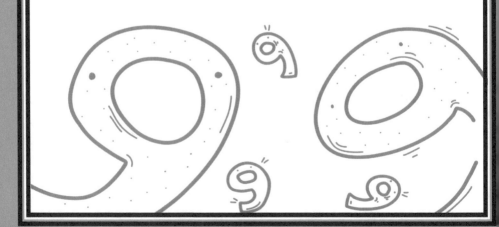

A WOULD YOU RATHER

HAVE A SPORTS CAR THAT BREAKS DOWN A LOT

AN OLD CAR THAT NEVER BREAKS DOWN?

B WOULD YOU RATHER

ONLY BE ABLE TO HAVE YOUR FAVORITE FOOD FROM NOW ON

NEVER EAT IT AGAIN?

WOULD YOU RATHER?
9 YEAR OLD
VERSION

(ASK THE OTHER PLAYER(S) TO
CHOOSE QUESTION 1 OR QUESTION 2)

A WOULD YOU RATHER

ONLY COMMUNICATE VIA DRAWINGS

 OR

ONLY COMMUNICATE WITH HAND GESTURES?

B WOULD YOU RATHER

KNOW EVERYONE AT SCHOOL

 OR

KEEP MEETING NEW PEOPLE?

WOULD YOU RATHER ?

9 YEAR OLD
VERSION

PLAYER 1

(ASK THE OTHER PLAYER(S) TO
CHOOSE QUESTION 1 OR QUESTION 2)

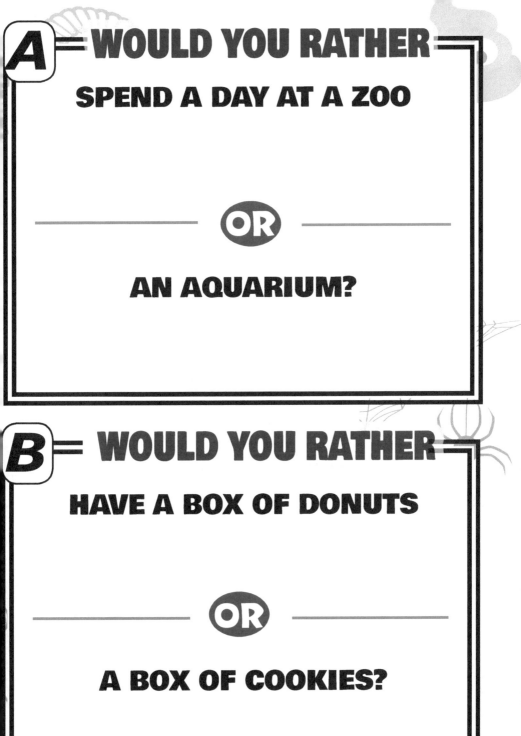

A — WOULD YOU RATHER
SPEND A DAY AT A ZOO

OR

AN AQUARIUM?

B — WOULD YOU RATHER
HAVE A BOX OF DONUTS

OR

A BOX OF COOKIES?

WOULD YOU RATHER?

9 YEAR OLD
VERSION

PLAYER 2

(ASK THE OTHER PLAYER(S) TO
CHOOSE QUESTION 1 OR QUESTION 2)

WOULD YOU RATHER

GO SLEDDING IN WINTER

 OR

SWIMMING IN SUMMER?

WOULD YOU RATHER

HAVE THE CHANCE TO SPEND A NIGHT IN A TENT

 OR

IN A CAMPER VAN?

WOULD YOU RATHER ?

9 YEAR OLD
VERSION

PLAYER 1

(ASK THE OTHER PLAYER(S) TO
CHOOSE QUESTION 1 OR QUESTION 2)

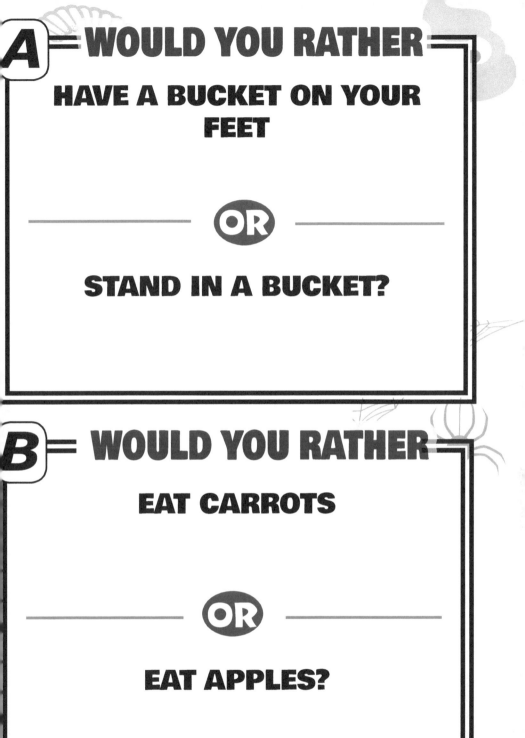

A — WOULD YOU RATHER

HAVE A BUCKET ON YOUR FEET

OR

STAND IN A BUCKET?

B — WOULD YOU RATHER

EAT CARROTS

OR

EAT APPLES?

WOULD YOU RATHER?
9 YEAR OLD
VERSION

PLAYER 2

(ASK THE OTHER PLAYER(S) TO
CHOOSE QUESTION 1 OR QUESTION 2)

A — WOULD YOU RATHER

HAVE THE CHANCE TO SPEND A NIGHT IN AN IGLOO

 OR

IN A TREEHOUSE?

B — WOULD YOU RATHER

SLEEP ON THE FLOOR

 OR

ON A MATTRESS THAT IS TOO SOFT?

WOULD YOU RATHER?
9 YEAR OLD
VERSION

PLAYER 1

(ASK THE OTHER PLAYER(S) TO
CHOOSE QUESTION 1 OR QUESTION 2)

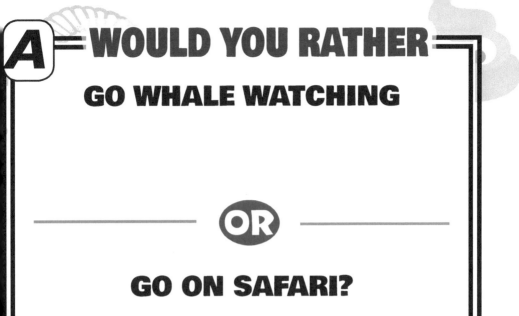

A | WOULD YOU RATHER

GO WHALE WATCHING

OR

GO ON SAFARI?

B | WOULD YOU RATHER

WEAR A SWIMMING COSTUME IN THE SNOW

A FUR COAT IN THE DESERT?

WOULD YOU RATHER?

9 YEAR OLD
VERSION

PLAYER 2

(ASK THE OTHER PLAYER(S) TO
CHOOSE QUESTION 1 OR QUESTION 2)

WOULD YOU RATHER

A

EAT YOUR FOOD OFF A PLATE ON THE FLOOR

 OR

OFF A TABLE WITHOUT A PLATE?

WOULD YOU RATHER

B

STAMP YOUR FEET WHENEVER YOU WALK

 OR

TIPTOE EVERYWHERE?

WOULD YOU RATHER ?

9 YEAR OLD
VERSION

PLAYER 1

(ASK THE OTHER PLAYER(S) TO
CHOOSE QUESTION 1 OR QUESTION 2)

A WOULD YOU RATHER

MOW THE LAWN

 OR

WASH THE CAR?

B WOULD YOU RATHER

PUT KETCHUP ON ICE CREAM

 OR

CHOCOLATE SAUCE ON PIZZA?

WOULD YOU RATHER?
9 YEAR OLD
VERSION

PLAYER 2

(ASK THE OTHER PLAYER(S) TO
CHOOSE QUESTION 1 OR QUESTION 2)

A | WOULD YOU RATHER

HAVE AN UGLY HOUSE

 OR

AN UGLY CAR?

B | WOULD YOU RATHER

HAVE A LARGE BACKYARD WITH NOTHING IN IT

 OR

A SMALL BACKYARD WITH SWINGS AND A SLIDE?

WOULD YOU RATHER ?
9 YEAR OLD
VERSION

PLAYER 1

(ASK THE OTHER PLAYER(S) TO
CHOOSE QUESTION 1 OR QUESTION 2)

A WOULD YOU RATHER

SKATEBOARD

 OR

ROLLERBLADE?

B WOULD YOU RATHER

HAVE TO WRITE WITH A CRAYON

 OR

A PERMANENT MARKER?

WOULD YOU RATHER?
9 YEAR OLD
VERSION

PLAYER 2

(ASK THE OTHER PLAYER(S) TO
CHOOSE QUESTION 1 OR QUESTION 2)

A = WOULD YOU RATHER

BE A GOOD RUNNER

 OR

A GOOD GYMNAST?

B = WOULD YOU RATHER

BE SO TALL YOU HAVE TO DUCK TO GO THROUGH DOORS

 OR

SO SHORT YOU CAN'T REACH THE COUNTER IN SHOPS?

WOULD YOU RATHER ?

9 YEAR OLD
VERSION

PLAYER 1

(ASK THE OTHER PLAYER(S) TO
CHOOSE QUESTION 1 OR QUESTION 2)

A WOULD YOU RATHER

ALWAYS HAVE TO CLEAN

 OR

ALWAYS HAVE TO COOK?

B WOULD YOU RATHER

HAVE TO HOLD YOUR PEN IN YOUR MOUTH TO WRITE

 OR

WITH YOUR FEET?

WOULD YOU RATHER ?
9 YEAR OLD
VERSION

PLAYER 2

(ASK THE OTHER PLAYER(S) TO
CHOOSE QUESTION 1 OR QUESTION 2)

A WOULD YOU RATHER

HAVE TO WALK AROUND ALL DAY IN HIGH HEELS

 OR

GIANT CLOWN SHOES?

B WOULD YOU RATHER

HAVE NO TV

 OR

NO COMPUTER?

WOULD YOU RATHER?

9 YEAR OLD
VERSION

PLAYER 1

(ASK THE OTHER PLAYER(S) TO
CHOOSE QUESTION 1 OR QUESTION 2)

A | WOULD YOU RATHER

BE A SQUIRREL

 OR

A BAT?

B | WOULD YOU RATHER

LIVE ON THE TOP FLOOR OF A TALL BUILDING WITH AMAZING VIEWS

 OR

THE BOTTOM FLOOR WITH A GARDEN?

WOULD YOU RATHER?
9 YEAR OLD
VERSION

PLAYER 2

(ASK THE OTHER PLAYER(S) TO
CHOOSE QUESTION 1 OR QUESTION 2)

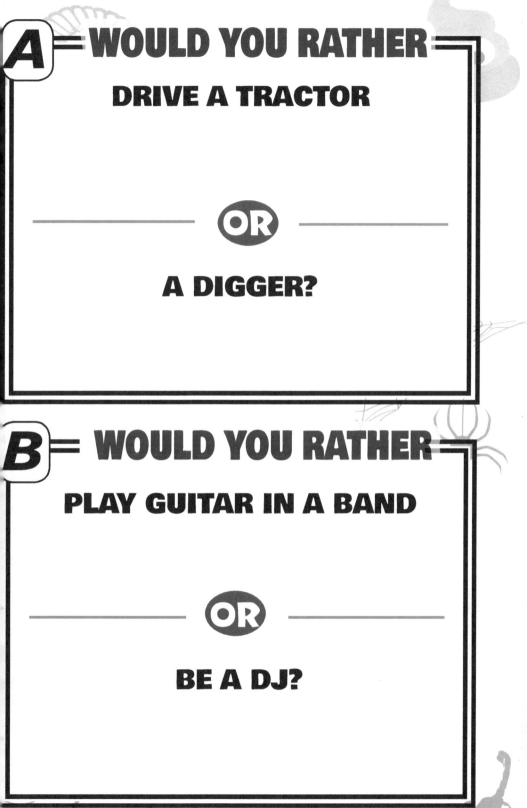

A — WOULD YOU RATHER

DRIVE A TRACTOR

OR

A DIGGER?

B — WOULD YOU RATHER

PLAY GUITAR IN A BAND

OR

BE A DJ?

WOULD YOU RATHER ?
9 YEAR OLD
VERSION

PLAYER 1

(ASK THE OTHER PLAYER(S) TO
CHOOSE QUESTION 1 OR QUESTION 2)

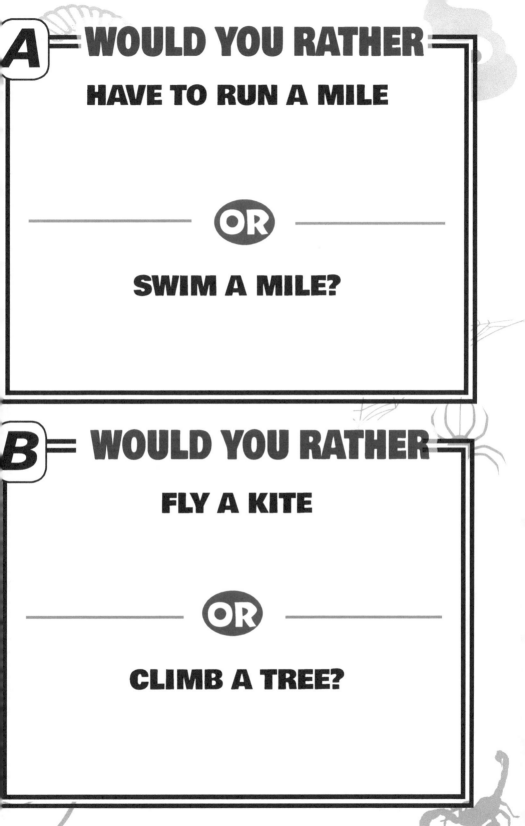

A WOULD YOU RATHER

HAVE TO RUN A MILE

OR

SWIM A MILE?

B WOULD YOU RATHER

FLY A KITE

OR

CLIMB A TREE?

WOULD YOU RATHER?
9 YEAR OLD
VERSION

PLAYER 2

(ASK THE OTHER PLAYER(S) TO
CHOOSE QUESTION 1 OR QUESTION 2)

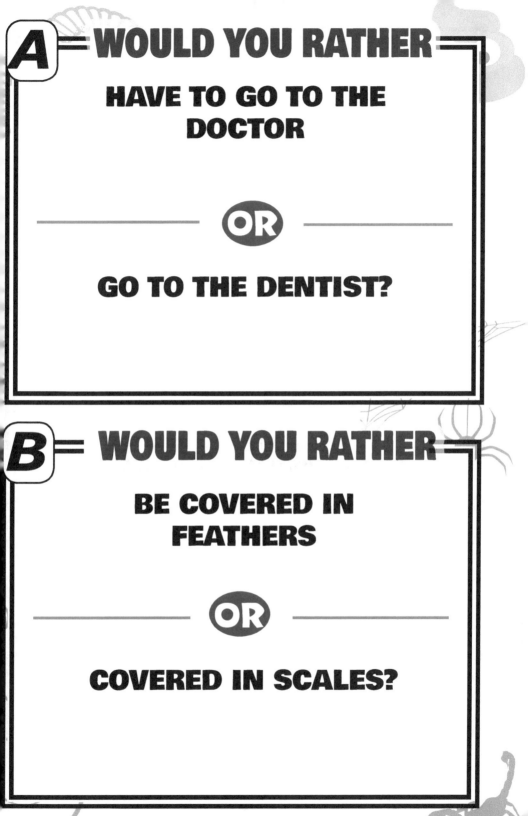

A — WOULD YOU RATHER

HAVE TO GO TO THE DOCTOR

OR

GO TO THE DENTIST?

B — WOULD YOU RATHER

BE COVERED IN FEATHERS

OR

COVERED IN SCALES?

WOULD YOU RATHER?
9 YEAR OLD
VERSION

PLAYER 1

(ASK THE OTHER PLAYER(S) TO
CHOOSE QUESTION 1 OR QUESTION 2)

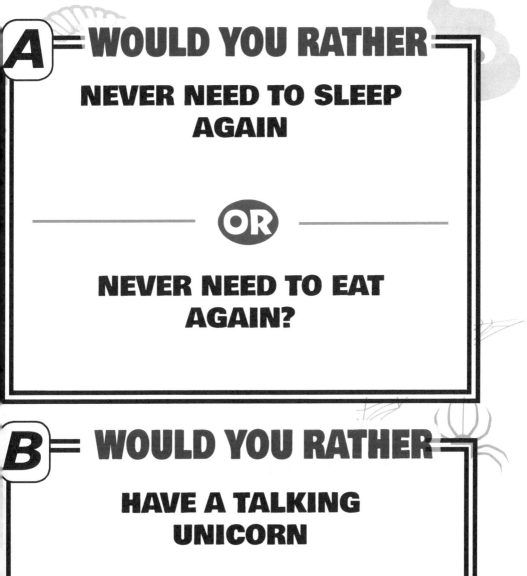

A — WOULD YOU RATHER

NEVER NEED TO SLEEP AGAIN

OR

NEVER NEED TO EAT AGAIN?

B — WOULD YOU RATHER

HAVE A TALKING UNICORN

OR

A PEGASUS?

WOULD YOU RATHER ?

9 YEAR OLD
VERSION

PLAYER 2

(ASK THE OTHER PLAYER(S) TO
CHOOSE QUESTION 1 OR QUESTION 2)

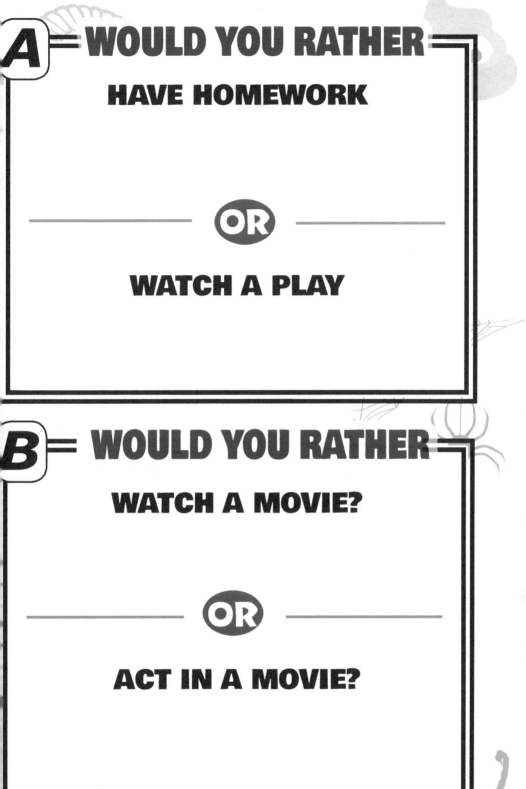

WOULD YOU RATHER

A

HAVE HOMEWORK

OR

WATCH A PLAY

WOULD YOU RATHER

B

WATCH A MOVIE?

OR

ACT IN A MOVIE?

WOULD YOU RATHER ?
9 YEAR OLD
VERSION

PLAYER 1

(ASK THE OTHER PLAYER(S) TO
CHOOSE QUESTION 1 OR QUESTION 2)

A | WOULD YOU RATHER

STROKE A SNAKE

OR

HOLD A TARANTULA?

B | WOULD YOU RATHER

FALL OUT WITH YOUR BEST FRIEND

OR

HAVE TO SPEND A DAY WITH YOUR WORST ENEMY?

WOULD YOU RATHER ?
9 YEAR OLD
VERSION

PLAYER 2

(ASK THE OTHER PLAYER(S) TO
CHOOSE QUESTION 1 OR QUESTION 2)

A  WOULD YOU RATHER

HAVE FLOORS COVERED IN STICKY GUM

 OR

CEILINGS DRIPPING DIRTY WATER?

B WOULD YOU RATHER

PLAY OUTSIDE

 OR

SIT INSIDE READING A BOOK?

WOULD YOU RATHER?
9 YEAR OLD
VERSION

PLAYER 1

(ASK THE OTHER PLAYER(S) TO
CHOOSE QUESTION 1 OR QUESTION 2)

A

WOULD YOU RATHER

BE IN A ROOM FULL OF BALLOONS

OR

A ROOM WITH BOUNCY WALLS AND FLOORS?

B

WOULD YOU RATHER

GO BUNGEE JUMPING

OR

GO GO-KARTING?

WOULD YOU RATHER?
9 YEAR OLD
VERSION

PLAYER 2

(ASK THE OTHER PLAYER(S) TO
CHOOSE QUESTION 1 OR QUESTION 2)

A WOULD YOU RATHER

HAVE A DOG-SIZED MOUSE

A MOUSE-SIZED DOG?

B WOULD YOU RATHER

ALWAYS HAVE SOMETHING STUCK IN YOUR TEETH

STUCK IN YOUR EYE?

WOULD YOU RATHER?
9 YEAR OLD
VERSION

PLAYER 1

(ASK THE OTHER PLAYER(S) TO
CHOOSE QUESTION 1 OR QUESTION 2)

A — WOULD YOU RATHER

HAVE TO SNEEZE EVERY TIME YOU SAY HELLO

OR

LAUGH EVERY TIME YOU SAY GOODBYE?

B — WOULD YOU RATHER

ACCIDENTALLY STUB YOUR TOE

OR

GET HIT IN THE FACE WITH A FOOTBALL?

WOULD YOU RATHER?
9 YEAR OLD
VERSION

PLAYER 2

(ASK THE OTHER PLAYER(S) TO
CHOOSE QUESTION 1 OR QUESTION 2)

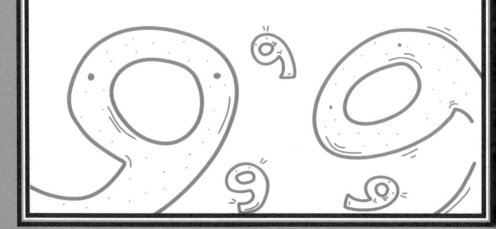

WOULD YOU RATHER

ALWAYS HAVE TO SAY WHAT YOU ARE THINKING

 OR

NEVER SPEAK AGAIN?

WOULD YOU RATHER

LOSE A FINGER

 OR

LIVE THE REST OF YOUR LIFE WITH A HEADACHE?

WOULD YOU RATHER?
9 YEAR OLD
VERSION

PLAYER 1

(ASK THE OTHER PLAYER(S) TO
CHOOSE QUESTION 1 OR QUESTION 2)

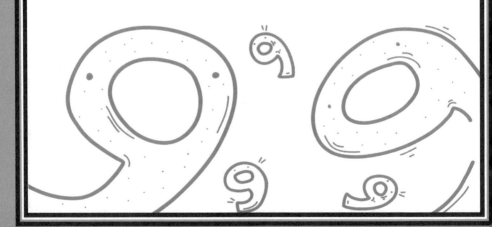

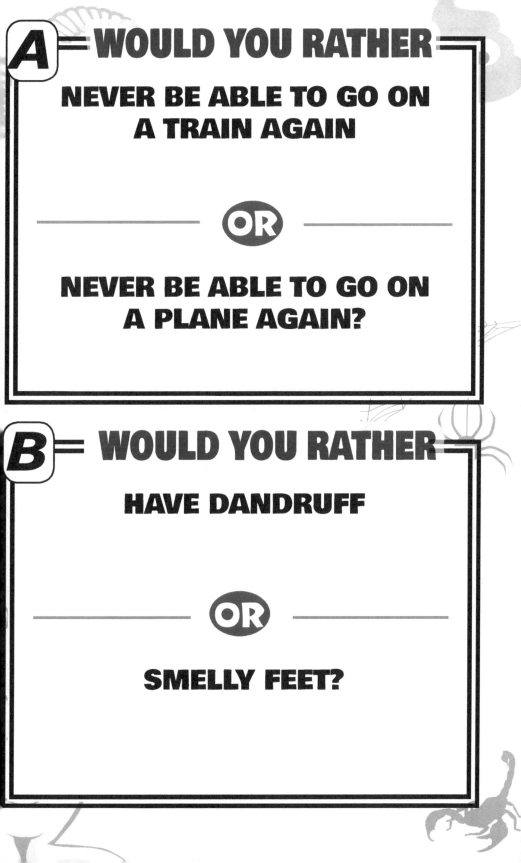

A WOULD YOU RATHER

NEVER BE ABLE TO GO ON A TRAIN AGAIN

OR

NEVER BE ABLE TO GO ON A PLANE AGAIN?

B WOULD YOU RATHER

HAVE DANDRUFF

OR

SMELLY FEET?

WOULD YOU RATHER?
9 YEAR OLD
VERSION

PLAYER 2

(ASK THE OTHER PLAYER(S) TO
CHOOSE QUESTION 1 OR QUESTION 2)

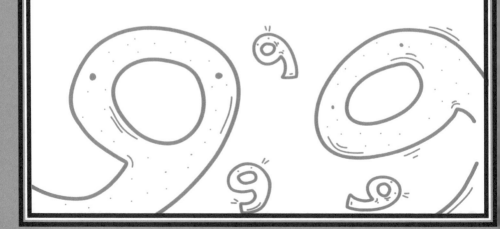

A WOULD YOU RATHER

WEAR SOMEONE ELSE'S SWEATY SHOES

 OR

WALK AROUND A PUBLIC BATHROOM BAREFOOT?

B WOULD YOU RATHER

HAVE SMARTER FRIENDS

 OR

BETTER-LOOKING FRIENDS?

WOULD YOU RATHER ?
9 YEAR OLD
VERSION

PLAYER 1

(ASK THE OTHER PLAYER(S) TO
CHOOSE QUESTION 1 OR QUESTION 2)

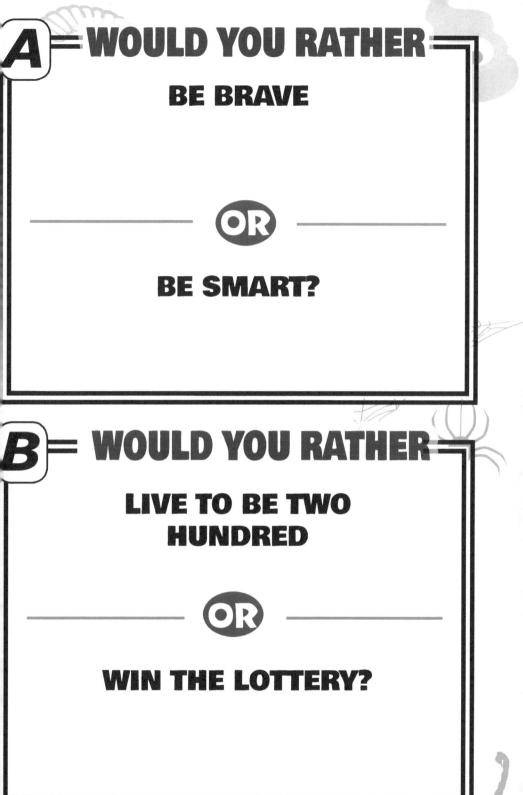

A — WOULD YOU RATHER

BE BRAVE

OR

BE SMART?

B — WOULD YOU RATHER

LIVE TO BE TWO HUNDRED

OR

WIN THE LOTTERY?

WOULD YOU RATHER?
9 YEAR OLD
VERSION

PLAYER 2

(ASK THE OTHER PLAYER(S) TO
CHOOSE QUESTION 1 OR QUESTION 2)

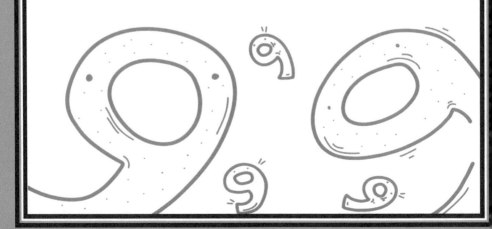

WOULD YOU RATHER

A

SEE A VOLCANO ERUPT

 OR

SEE A METEOR HIT THE EARTH?

WOULD YOU RATHER

B

WAKE UP WITH NO EYEBROWS

 OR

NO FINGERNAILS?

WOULD YOU RATHER ?
9 YEAR OLD
VERSION

PLAYER 1

(ASK THE OTHER PLAYER(S) TO
CHOOSE QUESTION 1 OR QUESTION 2)

A WOULD YOU RATHER

EAT PIZZA

OR

LASAGNE?

B WOULD YOU RATHER

BE ABLE TO ALTER THE PAST

OR

SEE THE FUTURE?

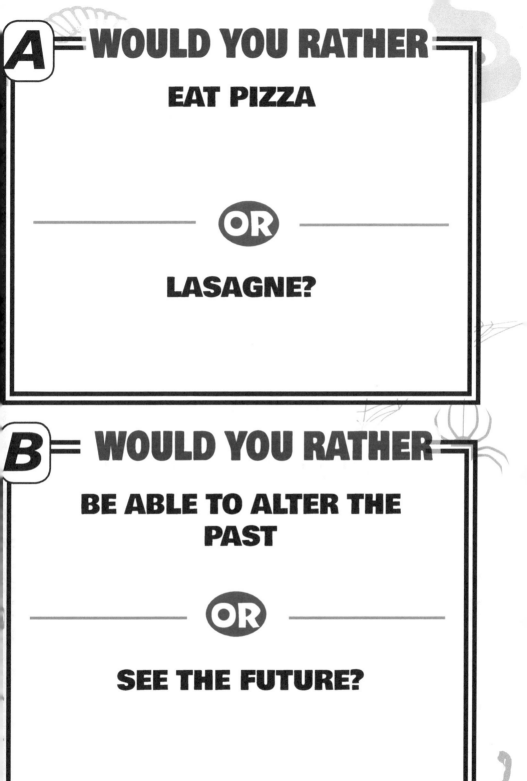

WOULD YOU RATHER?

9 YEAR OLD
VERSION

PLAYER 2

(ASK THE OTHER PLAYER(S) TO
CHOOSE QUESTION 1 OR QUESTION 2)

A — WOULD YOU RATHER

HAVE THREE BIG EYES
IN THE MIDDLE OF YOUR
HEAD

 OR

TWO BIG POINTY NOSES
ON YOUR CHIN ?

B — WOULD YOU RATHER

HAVE A MAGIC CARPET
THAT FLIES WHERE YOU
WANT

 OR

A CAR THAT CAN TAKE
YOU BACK IN TIME

Made in United States
Troutdale, OR
09/26/2023

13197506R00060